First Little Readers™

L

Pete Makes Pizza

by Liza Charlesworth

ISBN: 978-1-338-89050-1

Designer: Cynthia Ng; Illustrated by John Lund

Copyright © 2023 by Liza Charlesworth. All rights reserved. Published by Scholastic Inc.

1 2 3 4 5 6 7 8 9 10   68   31 30 29 28 27 26 25 24 23 22

Printed in Jiaxing, China. First printing, January 2023.

Meet a kid named Pete.
Pete only liked to do things
he was REALLY good at.
And Pete was great at catch.

So guess what?
Pete and his buddy Pam
played it a whole lot.
Throw, catch. Throw, catch.

What did Pete NOT like to do?
Take a chance and try new things!
So Pete wasn't happy when his mom said,
"Do you want to learn how to make pizza?"
"Well…um…I guess so," replied Pete.

First, Pete learned how to stretch out the dough.

Then, Pete learned how to pour on the tomato sauce.

Next, Pete learned how to sprinkle on A LOT of cheese…

…and a little bit of spice.
MMMMMMMMMMM!

Last, Pete learned how to put
the pizza in the oven to bake.
"Keep an eye on it," said his mom.
"Call me when the timer beeps in 15 minutes.
That means the pizza is ready to take out."

Pete sat in the kitchen
and waited for the timer to beep.
He was proud of himself
for trying something new.

After a while, his buddy Pam came by.
She yelled through the open window,
"Hey Pete, come play catch with me!"
"I can't leave the kitchen," he replied.
"I'm baking a pizza in the oven."

9

"Well, how about we play through
this open window then?" said Pam.
"I guess that will be OK," said Pete.
So, they did.
Throw, catch. Throw, catch.

Throw, catch. Throw, catch.
Pete had so much fun playing with Pam
that he didn't even hear
the timer go off.
BEEP, BEEP, BEEP!

11

BEEP, BEEP, BEEP!
Pete didn't smell smoke, but his mom did.
She raced into the kitchen and
took the pizza out of the oven.
It was burned, burned, burned!

"Sorry!" he cried. "I tried something new,
but it just didn't work out."
Pete let the pizza cool on the counter.
Then, he got so mad at himself
that he threw it right out the window.
And guess what?

13

His pal Pam caught it!
"Wow, I didn't know you could play catch
with a burned pizza," said Pete.
"See what can happen when you
try new things?" said his mom.

"Now, let's make a new pizza," she said.
"OK," he replied. "I won't let it burn."
And this time, Pete kept his word.
When the timer went *BEEP, BEEP, BEEP!*,
he shouted, "Mom, the pizza is ready!"
And she took it out of the oven.

15

MMMMMMMMMMMMMMMM!
Pete's pizza was perfect.
And he learned an important lesson:
Great stuff can happen when you
take a chance and try new things!